BATTLES OF THE AMERICAN CIVIL WAR

Catherine Clinton

Children's Press®
An imprint of Scholastic Inc.

Special thanks to our consultant, Dr. Le'Trice Donaldson, Assistant Professor of History, Auburn University, for making sure the text of the book is authentic and historically accurate.

Library of Congress Cataloging-in-Publication Data available
ISBN 978-1-5461-3634-7 (library binding) | ISBN 978-1-5461-3635-4 (paperback) |
ISBN 978-1-5461-3636-1 (ebook)

10 9 8 7 6 5 4 3 2 1 25 26 27 28 29

Printed in China 62
First edition, 2025

Design by Kathleen Petelinsek
Series produced by Spooky Cheetah Press

Front cover: Allan Pinkerton, President Lincoln, and Union general John A. McClernand, in Sharpsburg, Maryland, 1862

Back cover: The assault on Fort Wagner, 1863

Find the Truth!

Everything you are about to read is true ***except*** for one of the sentences on this page.

Which one is **TRUE**?

T or F The Confederate army never invaded the North.

T or F Ending slavery became a war aim in 1863.

Find the answers in this book.

What's in This Book?

The Civil War was the first military conflict to be photographed extensively.

Union soldiers get ready for battle.

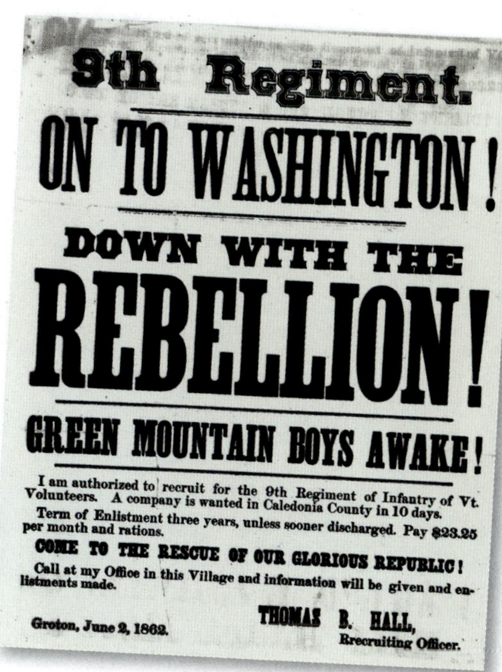

9th Regiment.

ON TO WASHINGTON!

DOWN WITH THE

REBELLION!

GREEN MOUNTAIN BOYS AWAKE!

I am authorized to recruit for the 9th Regiment of Infantry of Vt. Volunteers. A company is wanted in Caledonia County in 10 days.

Term of Enlistment three years, unless sooner discharged. Pay $23.25 per month and rations.

COME TO THE RESCUE OF OUR GLORIOUS REPUBLIC!

Call at my Office in this Village and information will be given and enlistments made.

Groton, June 2, 1862.

THOMAS B. HALL, Rrecruiting Officer.

A poster encouraging men to join the Union army

The American Civil War pitted the Union army against the Confederacy. This map shows the major battles of the war, all covered in this book.

An estimated 620,000 soldiers died in the Civil War.

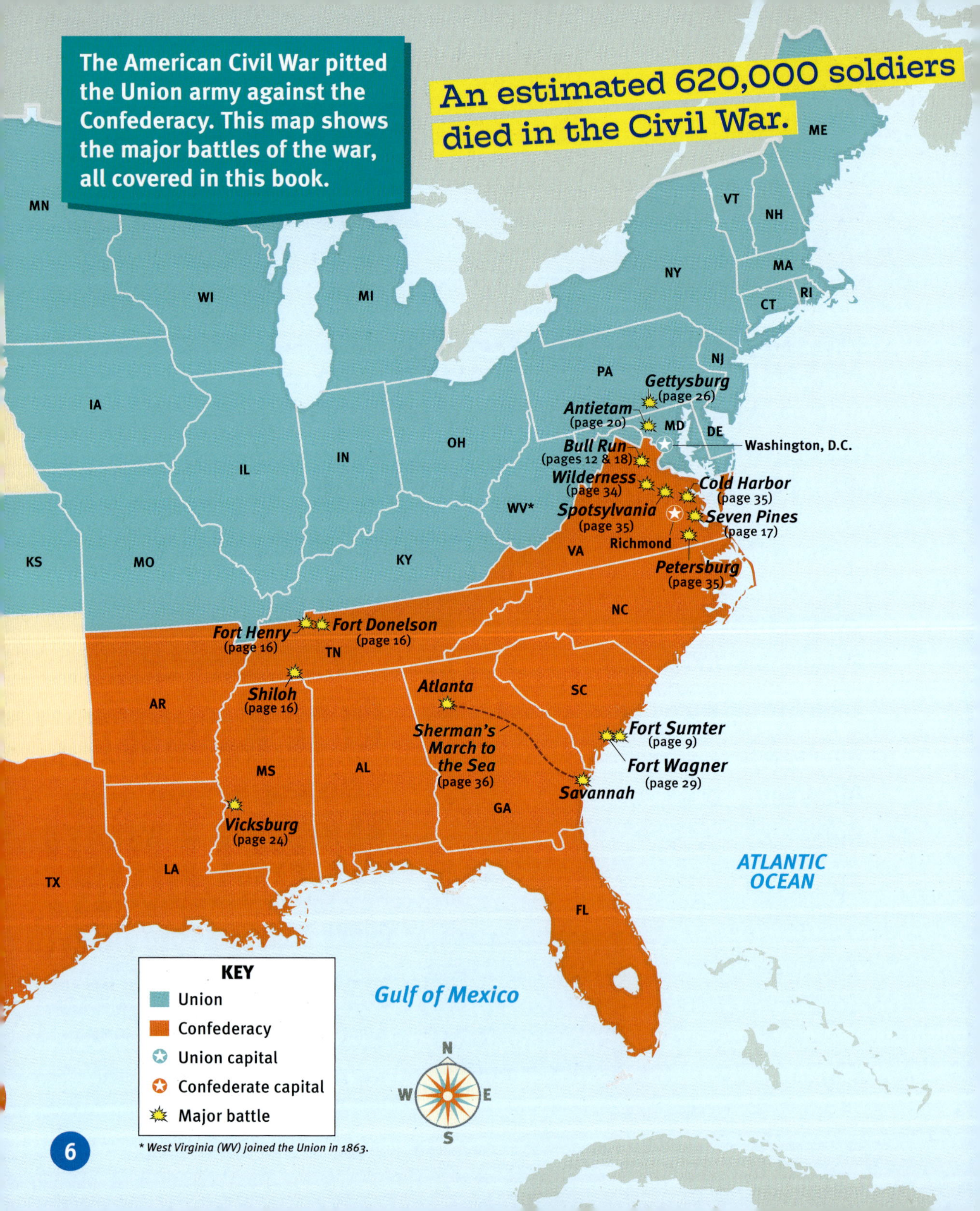

ME
VT
NH
MA
RI
CT
NY
NJ
PA
MN
WI
MI
IA
IL
IN
OH
MD
DE
WV*
KS
MO
KY
VA
NC
TN
SC
AR
MS
AL
GA
TX
LA
FL

Gettysburg (page 26)
Antietam (page 20)
Washington, D.C.
Bull Run (pages 12 & 18)
Wilderness (page 34)
Cold Harbor (page 35)
Spotsylvania (page 35)
Seven Pines (page 17)
Richmond
Petersburg (page 35)
Fort Henry (page 16)
Fort Donelson (page 16)
Shiloh (page 16)
Atlanta
Sherman's March to the Sea (page 36)
Fort Sumter (page 9)
Fort Wagner (page 29)
Savannah
Vicksburg (page 24)

ATLANTIC OCEAN

Gulf of Mexico

N
W
E
S

KEY
- Union
- Confederacy
- Union capital
- Confederate capital
- Major battle

* *West Virginia (WV) joined the Union in 1863.*

INTRODUCTION

In **1860**, the United States of America was nearing its centennial, or **100th anniversary**. But the unity of the states had never been more at risk. The institution of **slavery** **was tearing the country apart**.

The United States was growing. Most people in the **North did not want slavery** to spread to new territories. But most white people in the **South did**. The Republican Party had been formed in 1854 to **stop the spread of slavery**. In November 1860, **Republican Abraham Lincoln won the presidential election**. In December, South Carolina **seceded** and attempted to form a new country: the Confederate States of America, also known as the Confederacy. The rebellion would lead to the American Civil War, which threatened to tear the nation apart. Battles raged across the country as the **Union army of the United States** fought the **Confederate army** in an effort to keep the country together. That struggle would also decide the fate of four million enslaved people.

The Union named battles after nearby rivers. Confederates used nearby towns. For example, Confederates called the Battle of Bull Run the Battle of Manassas.

No one was killed during the attack on Fort Sumter. Two men died accidentally during the surrender.

CHAPTER

Insurrection

On April 12, 1861, the first shots of the Civil War were fired at Fort Sumter in Charleston, South Carolina. The conflict started when Confederates demanded that Union troops stationed there **evacuate** the fort. The Union soldiers refused. Shortly after, Confederate forces began a **bombardment** that lasted for 36 hours. The Union commander finally surrendered on April 13. By June of that year, 10 more Southern states had joined the rebellion. Both sides hurried to ready themselves for more battles to come.

Calls to War

On April 15, President Lincoln issued a call for volunteers. Men in the North were eager to crush the rebellion. In Confederate states, they recruited men by calling on them to defend their property and preserve their way of life. People on both sides of the conflict thought the war would not last long. They were proven wrong.

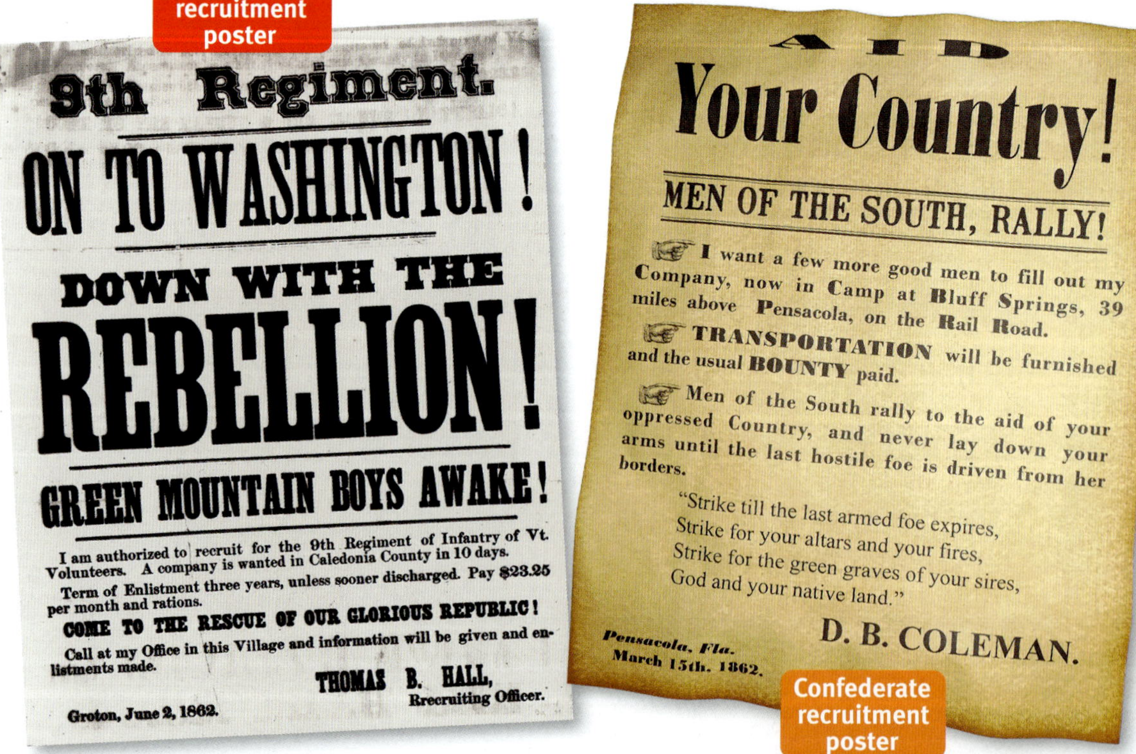

The Union usually wore blue uniforms. The Confederacy's were gray. But there were no standard uniforms, especially at the beginning of the war.

Union soldiers were called Yankees. Confederates were called Rebels.

Going on the Offensive

President Lincoln was anxious to bring the war to a quick end. The Army of the Potomac was the main body of the Union army in the East. In July, Lincoln ordered that unit to capture the Confederate **capital** of Richmond, Virginia. The troops started out from Washington, D.C., accompanied by residents who thought it would be fun to watch a battle. They did not make it very far before they met up with Confederate forces at Bull Run Creek near Centerville, Virginia.

FIRST BATTLE OF BULL RUN CONFEDERATE VICTORY
JULY 21, 1861
CASUALTIES:
Union: 2,896
Confederate: 1,982

The Battle of Bull Run

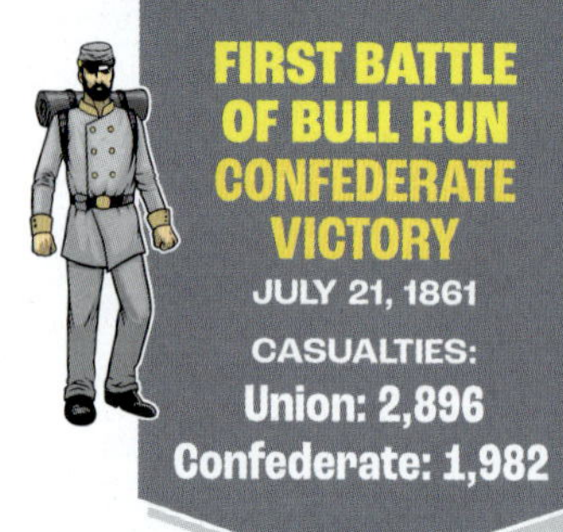

Fighting began on July 21. At first, the Union troops had the advantage. The Confederate army was forced to **retreat**. However, the Union general failed to press the advantage, and the Rebels rallied. As the Union army fled the battlefield, they were hindered by the civilians who were also scattering in a panic. When the Union army finally made it back to Washington, D.C., Lincoln fired its commanding officer.

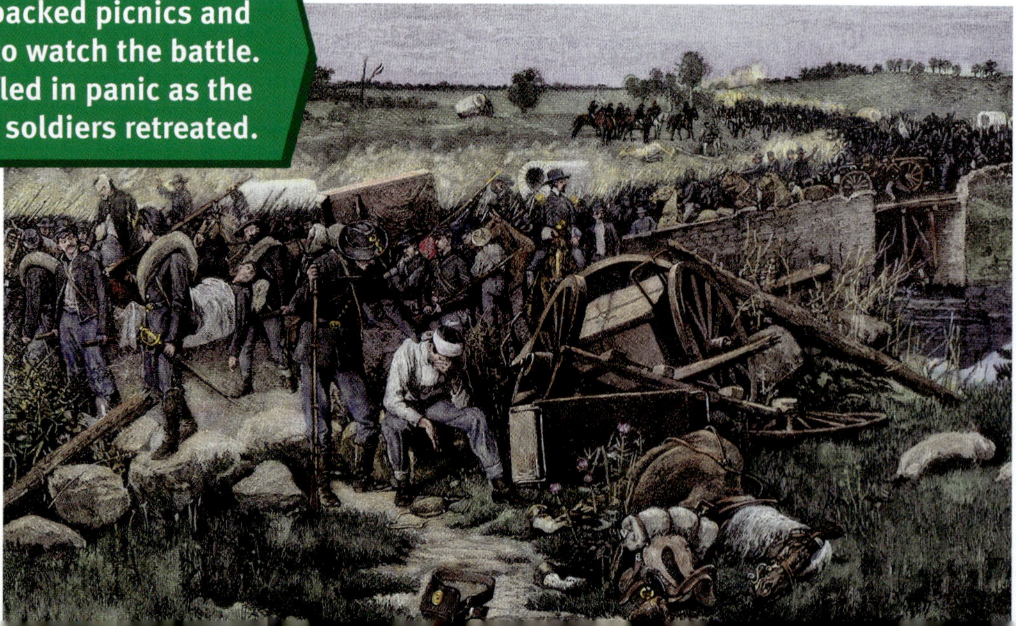

People from Washington, D.C., packed picnics and went to watch the battle. They fled in panic as the Union soldiers retreated.

Help for Soldiers

After the Battle of Bull Run, a New York women's organization called WCAR (which stands for Women's Central Association of Relief) saw how few medical supplies the Union army had. They met with President Lincoln to create an organization to help set up military hospitals and help transport wounded soldiers. They also handed out medical supplies, food, and clothing to those who needed them. That organization was called the U.S. Sanitary Commission. It played a key role in helping soldiers on both sides throughout the war.

This lodge in Alexandria, Virginia, was for disabled soldiers.

Union-issued boots were the first footwear to differentiate between right and left.

Nearly 200,000 new volunteers rushed to Washington, D.C., after the Union's defeat at Bull Run.

The Union army often built bridges out of boats to cross rivers.

CHAPTER 2

The Hard Hand of War

People were shocked by the death toll of the Battle of Bull Run. It suddenly became clear that the war might be a long, bloody struggle. Soon after the battle, President Lincoln put General George B. McClellan in charge of the Army of the Potomac in the East. As 1862 got underway, attention turned to the western theater of operations. The army of the West under Union general Ulysses S. Grant was having more success than the army in the East.

BATTLE OF SHILOH UNION VICTORY
APRIL 6–7, 1862
CASUALTIES:
Union: 13,047
Confederate: 10,669

Hard-Won Victories

In February, Grant captured Fort Henry on the Tennessee River and Fort Donelson on the Cumberland River. Two main supply routes for the Rebels were now under Union control.

Then, on April 6, 1862, Confederate forces attacked the Union troops at Pittsburg Landing in Tennessee. For 12 hours, the Union soldiers were battered and beaten back. **Reinforcements** arrived later in the day and the Union was able to force a Confederate retreat. The victory came at a huge cost.

Grant's troops were camped near a small church called Shiloh when they were attacked. Shiloh is a biblical term that means "place of peace."

The Battle of Shiloh

The two armies met at a crossroads called Seven Pines.

The Battle of Seven Pines

In the east, the Army of the Potomac was marching toward Richmond again. The soldiers clashed with the main Confederate army in the east—the Army of Northern Virginia—on May 31 in Fair Oaks Station, Virginia. After a day of fighting, neither side could claim victory, but the battle had a huge impact on the rest of the war. The commander of the Army of Northern Virginia was badly wounded in the fight and was later replaced by General Robert E. Lee.

Here, enslaved people take advantage of the battle to escape behind Union lines.

The Second Battle of Bull Run

By August 28, fighting had moved north. Once again, the two sides met at Bull Run. And once again the Union army failed to take advantage of its early success to deal a crushing blow to the Rebels. After more than two days of fighting, the greatly outnumbered Confederate troops had forced the Union army to retreat across Bull Run Creek.

The Wartime President

It is uncommon for a U.S. president to actively participate in the day-to-day operations of a war. But Abraham Lincoln was different. Thanks to the availability of the **telegraph**, Lincoln was in contact with his generals throughout the war and often advised them on strategy. This was especially important in the theater of the East, where Lincoln replaced the commander of the Army of the Potomac four times. He had to find a general who shared his vision for the war—and who would act quickly and decisively.

Lincoln visited battlefields to meet with his generals.

Lincoln slept in a cot in the telegraph office during battles so he could communicate with commanders in the field.

This photo of the Union army headquarters was taken the day before the Battle of Antietam.

The Battle of Antietam

The Confederate victory at the second battle of Bull Run inspired Lee to launch an invasion into Union territory. On September 14, the two sides met at South Mountain, near Frederick, Maryland. The Union troops forced Lee's men to retreat. The Confederate army did not return to Virginia, though. Instead, Lee set up a defensive line around Antietam Creek in Sharpsburg and waited for the Union army to arrive.

On September 17, the two sides faced off in a battle that lasted all day. When the fighting ended, more than 20,000 men lay wounded or dead. On the evening of September 18, Lee retreated to Virginia. The Union commander failed to go after Lee's retreating forces. Lincoln was angry. He felt that the Union might have been able to destroy Lee's army at that point. He would soon appoint a new general to lead the army in the East.

Photos of the dead after the Battle of Antietam shocked the nation.

Antietam is the deadliest single-day battle in American history.

At first, the war was fought to squash the rebellion and preserve the Union. Ending slavery became a war aim in 1863.

This illustration shows African American people greeting Lincoln in Washington, D.C., after the Emancipation Proclamation was issued in 1863.

CHAPTER 3

Turning the Tide

On January 1, 1863, President Lincoln signed the Emancipation Proclamation. It said that because Rebel states had not returned to the Union, the enslaved people in those states were now free. Ending slavery became a reason for fighting. With a new commander in charge of the Union army in the East and General Grant continuing to make progress in the west, Lincoln had high hopes for 1863. The Confederacy, on the other hand, was short on men, food, and supplies. Lee could not afford to let this war drag on too much longer.

Union cannons outside Vicksburg

The Siege and Fall of Vicksburg

In the western theater, Union troops had reached Vicksburg, Mississippi, in May. After attacks produced heavy **casualties**, Grant decided to lay **siege** to the city. For six weeks, Union **artillery** bombarded Vicksburg while its citizens hid in caves and nearly starved to death. On July 4, Confederate general John C. Pemberton's troops surrendered to General Grant.

Guerrilla Warfare

Some of the men who fought in the Civil War were called "guerrillas." They were not officially part of either army. They didn't fight in the battles. They roamed the Midwest, murdering and stealing. And though they weren't enlisted in either army, they did pick sides.

William Clarke Quantrill and William T. "Bloody Bill" Anderson were two notorious fighters who carried out raids against the Union army and those who supported the Union cause.

In 1863, Quantrill's raiders attacked the **abolitionist** town of Lawrence, Kansas, killing 150 people and burning most of the town. The next year, Anderson led the Centralia Massacre. He and his men pulled more than 20 unarmed Union soldiers off a train and killed them.

The destruction of Lawrence, Kansas

Gettysburg, Pennsylvania, is the farthest north the Confederate army made it into Union territory.

Union troops set up their defensive position.

The Battle of Gettysburg: Day 1

By the end of June, parts of both the Union and Confederate armies were in Pennsylvania. One of the most important battles of the war was about to start. The two sides met early in the morning on July 1. The Union soldiers were pushed back through the town of Gettysburg and took up a position on Cemetery Hill. Near midnight more than 90,000 reinforcements arrived.

The Battle of Gettysburg: Day 2

The Union soldiers formed a defensive line along the ridges and hills south of the town. In the afternoon on July 2, General Lee launched his assault. Fighting raged in locations that are now famous in American history: Devil's Den, Little Roundtop, and the Peach Orchard. Despite suffering heavy losses, the Union soldiers managed to hold their line.

When soldiers ran out of ammunition, many battles, like the one in Gettysburg, came down to hand-to-hand combat.

BATTLE OF GETTYSBURG UNION VICTORY
JULY 1–JULY 3, 1863
CASUALTIES:
Union: 23,000
Confederate: 28,000

The Battle of Gettysburg: Day 3

After two days of fighting, Lee assumed his enemy was severely weakened. He decided to try a full-frontal assault on the center of the Union line at Cemetery Ridge. In what came to be known as Pickett's Charge, 12,500 Confederate soldiers faced unrelenting rifle and artillery fire. About 7,500 of them were killed. Lee retreated to Virginia—and the Union army did not pursue. Lincoln was desperate for a commander who was not afraid to fight.

The Union victory at Gettysburg was a turning point in the war.

Today there is a national cemetery at Gettysburg.

The assault on Fort Wagner

Assault on Fort Wagner

On July 16, Union colonel Robert Gould Shaw and the men of the all-Black 54th Massachusetts regiment were chosen to lead the assault on the fort that guarded the entrance to Charleston Harbor in South Carolina. The men faced withering cannon fire as they attacked. The deaths of hundreds of soldiers, including Shaw, convinced Union commanders that the fort could not be taken by a frontal assault. Although the Confederates retained control of the fort, the assault showed the courage and fighting skill of Black soldiers.

Diversity in the Ranks

Historians estimate that almost four million soldiers fought in the Civil War. The vast majority of those were white men. However, Black and Native American soldiers served as well. So did women.

BLACK TROOPS

From the start of the war, activists such as Frederick Douglass and Martin Delany urged President Lincoln to allow Black men to fight for the Union. After July 1862, when Black men were allowed to enlist, both activists helped recruit Black soldiers, and Delany served as a doctor in the all-Black 54th Massachusetts. In 1865, he became the first Black officer in the U.S. Army. Major Delany also worked to recruit and train formerly enslaved men. In all, almost 200,000 Black men served in the army and the navy.

Background image: The 54th Massachusetts is one of the most famous Black regiments of the Civil War.

NATIVE AMERICAN SOLDIERS

About 3,500 Native American men, such as Henry Rice Hill (pictured), served in the Union army. Even more served with the Confederacy, but the exact number is unknown. The ancestral homelands of the Cherokee, Chickasaw, Choctaw, Muscogee (Creek), and Seminole nations were located in the Southeast. Those lands had been stolen from them in the 1830s and 1840s. During the war, they signed treaties with the Confederate government that guaranteed them land west of the Mississippi River if the Rebels won the war. Some members of those nations were enslavers, which also aligned them with the Confederate cause.

Kids served too. As many as 20 percent of the soldiers in the Civil War were under the age of 18.

WOMEN IN COMBAT

Women were forbidden from enlisting in both the Union and Confederate armies. Yet hundreds served as soldiers and as spies. Though the exact number is unknown, there are many documented cases of women who disguised themselves as men and enlisted under false names in order to fight. In many cases, the women's identities were only discovered if they were wounded or killed and their uniforms had to be removed. Some women, including Sarah Emma Edmonds (pictured), served for years without ever being discovered.

This illustration shows a meeting of Grant (left) and Lincoln.

Lincoln promoted Grant to lieutenant general—a rank that no other man besides George Washington had ever held.

CHAPTER

The Long Road to Peace

In March 1864, General Grant was put in charge of all the Union armies. General William Tecumseh Sherman took his place as commander of the Union forces in the West. The Union was ready to crush the Rebel armies. Grant would find and engage General Lee's Army of Northern Virginia and Sherman would make his way to Atlanta, Georgia. There, he was to engage and destroy the Army of Tennessee. Both tasks would claim the lives of thousands of soldiers.

Showdown in Virginia

On May 5, Lee's army attacked Union troops as they marched through an area known as the Wilderness near Chancellorsville, Virginia. For two days the soldiers fought among the trees and thick undergrowth of the forest. Fires created by the gunfire filled the area with smoke and intense heat. On the evening of May 6, the Union army began moving toward Spotsylvania. Lee, guessing Grant's intent, headed the same way.

Despite heavy losses in the Wilderness, Grant refused to retreat.

In this battle, many wounded soldiers were left to die because their comrades could not find them through the raging fires and billowing smoke.

This map shows Union and Confederate troop movements during Grant's Virginia Campaign.

The two sides clashed again at Spotsylvania on May 8. After 12 days of fighting and more than 30,000 casualties, there was no clear winner. On May 31 at Cold Harbor, the armies battled again. Grant lost about 7,000 men in a single hour. On June 15, Union troops arrived at Petersburg, where they settled in for a siege of the city.

Sherman took back Fort Sumter from the Confederates on February 22, 1865.

Sherman believed the only way to stop further thoughts of rebellion was to make the people in the South "feel the hard hand of war."

General Sherman's March to the Sea

Meanwhile, Sherman had been chasing Rebel troops from Chattanooga, Tennessee, south through Georgia. The Union soldiers fought many battles as they continued to their goal: the city of Atlanta. On September 2, 1864, the city fell. In November, Sherman started on his "March to the Sea," from Atlanta to Savannah. His troops burned homes and farms in an effort to convince civilians to abandon the Confederate cause.

Total War

The Civil War is often called a "total war." In part, that means that not only soldiers but also ordinary people were directly affected by it. This was true especially in the South, where most of the fighting took place. Many battles occurred right in people's farms and backyards. Armies took over people's homes. Sometimes houses were completely destroyed. In addition to losing their homes, people in the South struggled to find food. Battles ruined crops—and hungry soldiers often took whatever they could carry.

Atlanta, Georgia, lay in ruins at the end of the war.

Juneteenth is celebrated on June 19 as independence day for people who were held in bondage.

Surrender

The Confederates attempted one last assault on April 9, 1865. Then, finding himself surrounded, Lee requested a meeting with Grant. He surrendered at Appomattox Court House, Virginia. Over the coming weeks and months, the rest of the Confederate armies would follow suit. On June 19, Union soldiers arrived in Texas to announce that the war was over and that the enslaved people there were free.

Timeline: Milestones of the Civil War

APRIL 12, 1861
Confederate forces attack Fort Sumter. The American Civil War begins.

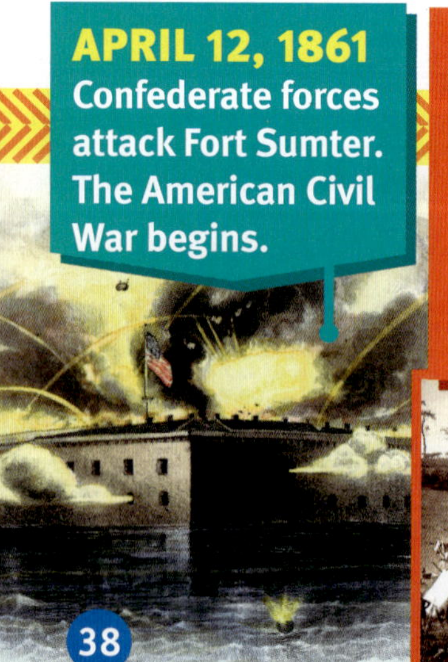

SEPTEMBER 17, 1862
The most deadly one-day battle in U.S. history takes place at Antietam.

JANUARY 1, 1863
The Emancipation Proclamation frees enslaved people living "within the rebellious states."

JULY 1–3, 1863
The Union victory at the Battle of Gettysburg turns the tide of the war.

An Uncertain Future

On April 14, President Lincoln and his wife celebrated General Lee's surrender by going to see a play at Ford's Theatre in Washington, D.C. While Lincoln watched the show, Confederate sympathizer John Wilkes Booth snuck up behind him and shot him in the head. Lincoln died the next day. The country had overcome a tremendous challenge in the Civil War. But another still remained—how to rebuild the nation. With Lincoln dead, the future of the United States was anything less than sure.

NOVEMBER 1864
General Sherman starts his "March to the Sea."

APRIL 9, 1865
General Lee (right) surrenders to General Grant (left).

NOVEMBER 6, 1865
The last Confederate troops surrender—by letter—after sailing their ship to England. The war is officially over.

People to Know

Ulysses S. Grant
(1822–1885)

Grant was born Hiram Ulysses Grant in Ohio. When he applied to the United States Military Academy at West Point, his name was mistakenly listed as Ulysses S. Grant, and he didn't bother changing it. After leading the Union armies to victory in the Civil War, Grant was elected president in 1868.

Robert E. Lee
(1807–1870)

Lee, who was born and raised in Virginia, graduated second in his class from West Point. In April 1861, President Lincoln offered Lee command of the Union forces. Instead, Lee resigned from the U.S. Army and joined the Confederacy. He explained, "Save in defence of my native State, I never desire again to draw my sword."

Ely Parker
(1828–1895)

Parker, a member of the Seneca Nation, was the highest-ranking Native American soldier in the Union army. As Grant's secretary, he drafted the terms of surrender. Parker went on to become the commissioner of Indian affairs—the person in charge of the U.S. government's relationship with Native American nations.

Robert Smalls
(1839–1915)

In 1861, Smalls was enslaved in South Carolina and working on a ship. In 1862, he managed to take the ship—with other enslaved crew members and their families—and sail it to a nearby Union navy fleet. Smalls turned the ship over and later became a captain in the navy. In 1874, he was elected to the U.S. Congress.

Susie King Taylor
(1848–1912)

Taylor, who was born into slavery in Georgia, liberated herself at age 14 during the war. Taylor served as a teacher and nurse in wartime South Carolina. She was the only Black woman to serve with the Union army and publish a memoir. Later in life, Taylor worked with an organization that helped female war veterans.

Elizabeth Van Lew
(1818–1900)

Van Lew was born in Richmond, Virginia, to a family of enslavers. But she was an abolitionist. After the war started, Van Lew dedicated herself to aiding Union prisoners of war and spying on the Confederacy. Her tombstone read: “She risked everything that is dear to man . . . that slavery might be abolished and the Union preserved.”

Eyewitness to History

Historians use primary sources to study the past. These are documents such as letters, manuscripts, diaries, photographs, and newspaper stories created during the time under study. Here are two primary sources from the Civil War that offer a glimpse of what life was like during that time.

A CONFEDERATE SOLDIER wrote to his wife describing conditions at Andersonville Prison—where Union prisoners of war were held. Here is an excerpt of the letter:

Yesterday One Hundred and Thirty Yankees died in the Hospitals, which is the maximum of deaths thus far in 24 Hours. They die from Diseases of the Digestive organs, such as Diarrhea, and Dysentery, brought on by the rude prison life, filth, and diet, also by scanty diet, with no variety, and many of them succomb to Hunger, not being accustomed to our Corn Homony (hominy), and the Confederate Government not having it in their power to furnish them wheat. The so-called Hospitals consist of low tents, in rows, the entire surrounded by a Stockade, and at present there are about 3000 Patients. As You stroll along these walks in the midst of human suffering, breathing the polluted atmosphere of disease in all its forms, the horrors of War can not be too strongly portrayed. At almost every step Death is busily engaged selecting his victims.

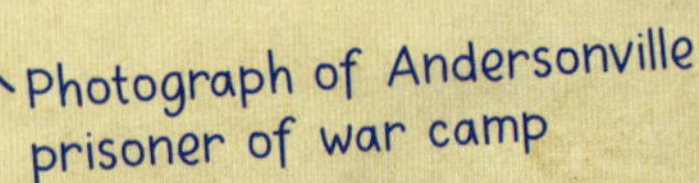

Photograph of Andersonville prisoner of war camp

BY THE SPRING OF 1863, many Southerners were facing starvation. Food was scarce, and the food that was available was too expensive for many to afford. On April 2, a group made up mostly of women attacked stores in Richmond and began grabbing food and other goods. Only when authorities threatened to shoot them did the women disperse. A Richmond woman wrote to a friend about what she saw before the riot:

An illustration of the riot that took place on April 2, 1863

As she raised her hand to remove her sunbonnet and use it for a fan, her loose calico sleeve slipped up and revealed the mere skeleton of an arm. She perceived my expression as I looked at it, and hastily pulled down her sleeve with a short laugh. "This is all that's left of me," she said. "It seems real funny, don't it?. . . We are starving. As soon as enough of us get together, we are going to the bakeries and each of us will take a loaf of bread. That is little enough for the government to give us after it has taken all our men."

True Statistics

How long the Civil War lasted: 4 years, 1 month, and 2 weeks

Estimated number of Union soldiers killed in battle: 110,100 (about 256,000 more died from diseases or in prison camps)

Estimated number of Union soldiers wounded in action: 275,174

Estimated number of Union prisoners of war: 30,192

Estimated number of Confederate soldiers killed in battle: 94,000 (about 164,000 more died from diseases)

Estimated number of Confederate soldiers wounded in action: 194,026

Estimated number of Confederate prisoners of war: 31,000

Did you find the truth?

F The Confederate army never invaded the North.

T Ending slavery became a war aim in 1863.

Resources

Other books in this series:

You can also look at:

Burton, Mark. *The American Civil War for Young Readers: The Greatest Battles and Most Heroic Events of the American Civil War*. Palm Springs, California: Curious Press, 2023.

Katz, Susan B. *The History of the Civil War: A History Book for New Readers*. Emeryville, California: Rockridge Press, 2021.

Lewer, Daniel. *Spies in the Civil War for Kids: A History Book*. Emeryville, California: Rockridge Press, 2021.

Patrick, Denise Lewis. *If You Lived During the Civil War*. New York: Scholastic, 2022.

Glossary

abolitionist (ab-uh-LISH-uh-nist) someone who worked to end slavery before and during the Civil War

artillery (ahr-TIL-ur-ee) large, powerful guns that are mounted on wheels or tracks

bombardment (bahm-BAHRD-muhnt) prolonged attack with bombs, missiles, or gunfire

capital (KAP-i-tuhl) the city where the government is based

casualties (KAZH-oo-uhl-teez) people who are injured or killed in a war

evacuate (i-VAK-yoo-ate) to move away from an area or building because it is dangerous there

reinforcements (ree-in-FORS-muhnts) extra troops sent to strengthen an army or other fighting force

retreat (ri-TREET) to withdraw from an attack

seceded (si-SEE-did) formally withdrew from the United States to form another country

siege (SEEJ) the surrounding of a place such as a city to cut off supplies and then wait for those inside to surrender

slavery (SLAY-vur-ee) the practice of holding people as property against their will, forcing them to work for no pay under threat of violence, and denying them the rights held by free persons

telegraph (TEL-i-graf) a device or system for sending messages over long distances using a code of electrical signals sent by wire or radio

Index

Page numbers in **bold** indicate illustrations.

About the Author

Catherine Clinton, who studied American history at Harvard and Princeton, is an award-winning author for young readers. She has written or edited more than 30 books. Her anthology *I, Too, Sing America* won the Claudia Lewis Bank Street Award. Clinton lives in San Antonio with her husband and a dog named Larry.

Photos ©: cover: Brady National Photographic Art Gallery/National Archives and Records Administration; back cover: Kurz & Allison/Library of Congress; 3: Everett Collection Historical/Alamy Images; 4: Alexander Gardner/Library of Congress; 5 top: Corbis/Getty Images; 5 bottom: Library of Congress/Corbis/VCG/Getty Images; 6–7: Jim McMahon/Mapman®; 8–9: North Wind Picture Archives/Alamy Images; 10 right: Library of Congress/Corbis/VCG/Getty Images; 11: Don Troiani. All Rights Reserved 2024/Bridgeman Images; 12 bottom: North Wind Pictures/Bridgeman Images; 13: National Library of Medicine; 14–15: Everett/Shutterstock; 16 bottom: Everett Collection Historical/Alamy Images; 17 main: Corbis/Getty Images; 19: Alexander Gardner/Library of Congress; 20 main: The Art Archive/Shutterstock; 21: Alexander Gardner/Library of Congress; 22–23: Bettmann/Getty Images; 24 main: Everett/Shutterstock; 25: Library of Congress; 26, 27: Don Troiani. All Rights Reserved 2024/Bridgeman Images; 28 bottom: eurobanks/Getty Images; 29 main: Kurz & Allison/Library of Congress; 30–31 background: Alamy Images; 31 top: Charles Van Schaick/Wisconsin Historical Society/Getty Images; 31 bottom: Fotosearch/Getty Images; 32: Science History Images/Alamy Images; 34: ClassicStock/Alamy Images; 35 main: Jim McMahon/Mapman®; 36: The Protected Art Archive/Alamy Images; 37: Selmar Rush Seibert/The LIFE Picture Collection/Shutterstock; 38 left: North Wind Picture Archives/Alamy Images; 38 center left: The Art Archive/Shutterstock; 38 center right: Universal History Archive/UIG/Shutterstock; 38 right: Don Troiani. All Rights Reserved 2024/Bridgeman Images; 39 left: Glasshouse Images/Shutterstock; 39 center: H. Armstrong Roberts/ClassicStock/Alamy Images; 39 right: The History Collection/Alamy Images; 40 top: Bettmann/Getty Images; 40 center: Gado/Getty Images; 40 bottom: Brady-Henfield-Colourisation Collection/Internet Archive; 41 top: Glasshouse Images/Shutterstock; 41 center: Gado/Getty Images; 41 bottom: Digital Image Library/Alamy Images; 42 right: Library of Congress; 43 center: Pictorial War Records/Battles of the Late Civil War in 1883/Encyclopedia of Alabama; 44: Universal History Archive/UIG/Shutterstock.

All other photos © Shutterstock.